MALCOLM IN THE MIDDLE™

THE HOSTAGE CRISIS

D0685002

BY TOM MASON & DAN DANKO

SCHOLASTIC INC.
New York   Toronto   London   Auckland   Sydney
Mexico City   New Delhi   Hong Kong   Buenos Aires

ISBN 0-439-23079-9

12 11 10 9 8 7 6 5 4 3 2 1   1 2 3 5 6/0
Printed in the U.S.A.
First Scholastic printing, July 2001

Y'know how when you're a kid, nothing ever really goes as planned?

Take me for instance. Except for the classes, I was having a good time in school. I had friends. I had people to eat lunch with. Homework was easy. Then somebody gave me an IQ test and it was all over.

Suddenly, I'm yanked out of my regular classes and stuck in with genius nerds called Krelboynes. They're so hopeless, their classroom is a trailer in back of the school. Right by the tetherball court.

Yep. I go to school in a mobile home. And I'm on the tetherball team.

It's like I'm a hostage to higher learning, a prisoner of Krelboynes.

CHAPTER ONE

"I think I'm going to be sick," I groaned. I held my stomach. I held my head. I groaned some more and pretended to gag. I dropped to my knees.

When I looked up, Stevie rolled his wheelchair to me, and started clapping. Stevie is, like, my best friend. He's got a round head like a basketball and I tease him that his big glasses make him look like an owl. His asthma makes every sentence last for hours, but he's the coolest of the Krelboynes, even if his parents are overprotective nuts. Plus, he has this awesome comic book collection in his bedroom.

"How was that?" I asked. "I call it 'Flu With Upset Stomach.'"

"You're ... not ... Bruce ... Willis," he wheezed. "But ... it ... could ... work."

Rehearsal is essential to any performance. You have to see the illness. *Be* the illness. Or something like that. I read it in *People* magazine.

I'm trying to fake sick. Not sick enough to be sent home or spend the day with the school nurse, but enough to get out of my next class.

It's all Hollywood's fault. They keep making these totally cool movies that I want to see, but I'm always stuck in school. By the time I get to the multiplex, the lines are too long and the movie's sold out anyway. I'm *not* going to be the last one to see it.

Kids should always be the first to see a movie. That way, we'll have something to talk about. Anything's better than yakking about school or whatever runny substance we're being force-fed at lunch.

I mean, given the choice between sitting in school listening to one of my classmates read *Hamlet* with the emotion of a nuclear physicist or sitting in a dark theater watching things blow up, which would you pick? You know I'm right.

The movie I want to see? That's the best part. It's *Predatory Aliens 6: This Time It's Personal*. Opening today at theaters everywhere.

If I can get out of my "Chemistry And You" class, I can snag some tickets for me and my friends before it sells out.

"Good ... luck," Stevie gasped. He turned and wheeled down the hallway as I shuffled into the classroom.

During roll call, I coughed out a weak "Here." I moaned as the teacher wrote the assignment on the wipe board. I moaned even louder when I got my beaker from the shelf.

"Is something wrong, Malcolm?" Mr. Heikenen asked. With his tiny wire-frame glasses, his big chalk-colored face and round, bald head he looked like a lightbulb on top of a lab coat. He spoke in such a monotone that even Einstein would have thought he was boring.

"No," I moaned pathetically. "I'll be all right. I think."

"That's the spirit," Mr. Heikenen said. "Concentrate on the chemistry lesson and your stomach pain will disappear!"

Some people take their science way too seriously.

We'd been in class for almost five minutes. My Bunsen burner was on. The fluid in my beaker was boiling rapidly. It was a good time to . . . flop. So I collapsed in a moaning pile on the floor. I opened one eye and looked around. No one cared. They all stared at their own beakers watching their fluids boil.

"I have captured the elusive gas, Mr. Heikenen!" a blond kid next to me yelled out. "We have achieved success!"

"Excellent," Mr. Heikenen enthused. "Write down your results and be ready to share them with the class."

What's wrong with having too many smart kids in one class? They pay attention, that's what. They do the assignment. This is so totally lame. I've got to get Francis to show me the symptoms for food poisoning again.

I picked myself off the floor but accidentally elbowed my beaker. It fell off the stand and crashed to the floor. Green liquid splat everywhere and totally melted through the floor.

Mr. Heikenen looked at me like I was a failed experiment. But where he saw disappointment, I saw opportunity.

"There's my experiment, Mr. Heikenen," I yelled. "I think it's worth a B+!"

He did not look happy as he pointed out the door. Janitor's office, here I come!

CHAPTER TWO

I left the Krelboyne trailer and went to the janitor's office. Actually, *office* is being too kind. It's more like a closet next to the gym. I don't know what Mr. Heikenen thinks the janitor can do.

He's going to need more than a mop and a bucket to clean up my latest effort. Maybe a haz-mat suit and a couple of two by fours.

"What is it this time?" the janitor grumbled. "Food fight? Broken water pipe? Upset stomach?"

"Nope," I boasted. "Chemical spill."

He groaned and slumped his shoulders. He'd already spent years cleaning up after Francis and Reese, and I wasn't making his life any easier. If he thinks it's been bad so far, just wait 'til he meets my little brother Dewey.

Stevie was waiting for me outside the computer lab.

"What . . . kept . . . you?" he gasped.

"Plan A and Plan B didn't work," I said. "I had to improvise. How'd *you* get out of class?"

He pointed to his wheelchair. "Suddenly . . . I . . . could . . . feel . . . my . . . legs," he chuckled.

"Very funny."

Stevie whipped out his cool Mac-compatible digital watch. "What . . . time . . . have . . . you . . . got?"

"0950." Military time. Stevie likes it when we act like spies. Me too.

"Let's . . . do . . . it!" Stevie exclaimed. He wheeled down the hallway, waving his arms like a drowning girl.

"Hee . . . eellpp!" he wheezed.

I opened to door to the computer lab and ran inside screaming, "Runaway wheelchair! Runaway wheelchair!"

The lab teacher jumped up from her seat like she was on fire. Well, like her butt was anyway. I pointed down the hall where Stevie was rolling away and she was gone. Hopefully Stevie can keep her running for the next five minutes and 38 seconds.

I looked around the class. There were only two kids in the room and they were busy staring at their screens like snakes stare at mice. I could've been a mass of stinky alien protoplasm and I don't think they would've cared. They were *downloading*.

I strolled casually to the teacher's computer. Checked my watch. Four minutes to go. I lifted her keyboard and found the "hidden" password. You'd think teachers would just memorize it or something, right? A couple of clicks of the mouse and Bang! I'm on a web site called GetYerTicketsHere.com.

First I had to click through all the ads to get to my

movie. Click. Click. Click. Click. And click. Three minutes to go.

Finally, I found the movie. Click. Click. First show after school? Sold out. Click. Next show? Gone. Click. The one after that? Click. Who are these people and why are they buying all of my tickets? My mom's probably behind this.

I looked at my watch. It had stopped. Okay, that's the last time I get a watch from a box of cereal. I don't care how many proofs-of-purchase they ask for. I didn't know how much time I had left, but I could hear my heart beating loud enough to burst out of my chest.

Is any movie that'll be on video in three months worth this kind of trouble?

You bet it is! Not only is this movie the biggest, coolest special effects extravaganza, like, ever, but you haven't lived until you've been to the movies with the Krelboynes.

Remember when you were little and you were afraid of the dark and thought there were monsters under your bed? Krelboynes never outgrew that. Take them to a scary movie and it's better than free candy or extra butter-flavoring. They hug their knees, hide their eyes behind jumbo popcorn tubs, and whisper "I want to go home! I want to go home!"

Sometimes it's better than the movie!

The only tickets that were available were for Saturday afternoon. That showtime's usually full of grandparents, mallrats, and kids whose parents need a couple of hours of peace and quiet.

Click!

And now it'll be filled with Krelboynes, too, thanks to my parents' credit card number.

I printed out the confirmation codes so we could get our tickets at the box office and grabbed them from the laser printer. I opened the door and bumped into Stevie and the teacher. Right on schedule. Whew!

"Stevie!" I said. "We were so worried. Are you okay?"

"Sorry . . . new . . . wheelchair . . . I . . . panicked . . . when . . . I . . . lost . . . control," Stevie said to the teacher. Stevie winked at me. I gave him my OK countersign. We were gold.

"That's okay, Stevie," the teacher consoled. "It happens to me whenever I get behind the wheel of a Camry."

At lunch, you'd have thought I was giving out SAT secrets. Dabney, Lloyd, Eraserhead, and Stevie couldn't wait for their codes.

"This is better than free cable," Lloyd said.

"Or being invisible," Eraserhead offered.

"There are over 350 different special effects shots in 93 minutes," Dabney said. "With 3.76344 effects per minute, it's on a par with any *Star Wars* rip-off."

"I've . . . waited . . . for . . . this . . . movie . . . ever . . . since . . . I . . . heard . . . about . . . it . . . on . . . the . . . Internet," Stevie excitedly gasped out.

"Seven bucks," I said. "Each."

"But these are for the matinee. They're only five dollars," Dabney complained.

"Let's do the math," I said. "There's my 'Get out of class early' fee, my 'Sneak into the computer lab' fee, and my 'High risk factor' fee. I'd say you're all getting off pretty easy."

They paid their money and I tore off their codes.

"I'll need a receipt," Dabney said. "For my taxes. Someday."

Stevie pressed a dollar bill into my hand and took his code number. "Stevie?" I asked. "What's this?"

"My . . . discount.   You . . . forgot . . . my . . . wheelchair . . . usage . . . fee," he wheezed as he rolled away.

There goes my popcorn money. I can do math in my head, I just can't own my own business yet.

CHAPTER THREE

"**H**onestly, Malcolm, what am I going to do with you?" Mom said when I finally got home.

She knows. She totally knows about my chemistry accident. How does she do that? Can she smell hydrochloric acid on me?

My mom kind of looks like a regular mom except for that constantly frazzled expression. Unless she's mad at one of us, which is, like, all the time. Then her eyes get that red Terminator glow and look like they could burn through steel.

She's got a lot to deal with, though. There's my dad who's so hairy she has to shave his back. My oldest brother Francis is away at military school. My other older brother, Reese, is a total Darwinian reject. And my baby brother Dewey is, well, Dewey.

"Honestly, Mom, I don't know what's gotten into Malcolm these days," Reese said. "Maybe his IQ is dropping."

Or maybe my brother ratted me out. Reese may be my older brother, but we're not anything alike. He's got a square head, a bad haircut, and a brain that just figured out the difference between fork and spoon. Think I'm joking? You should have seen him try to eat cereal last week.

None of that matters, though. I have a ticket to *Predatory Aliens 6* and he doesn't. All I have to do is get through Friday night and one more family dinner.

"How was school today, son?" That's my dad. You can recognize him 'cause he asks that question every night at dinner, usually while reaching for a roll. He never takes his eyes off the food while talking.

"Malcolm tried to melt the school," Reese smiled. "Everybody was talking about it. I'm surprised he didn't go to prison."

"Ahhh," Dad reminisced as he leaned back in his chair. "I remember when I used to get in trouble at school. Oh, the times I had —"

"Hal!" Mom scolded.

Dad stopped and looked at me. "Homework tonight," he said as he buttered his roll. "And I'll be checking your answers."

I glared at Reese. He happily ate more canned spaghetti, secure in the knowledge that he had ruined my evening again.

That's why, after dinner, I was sitting at the kitchen table scrawling out my homework instead of watching TV with Reese. But that's okay. If I can get my homework out of the way early, then there's nothing to keep me from seeing —

"So, what's this movie about?" Mom asked. Not

only did she successfully sneak up on me, but she knew about the movie? Are moms psychic? Of course they are, but I sensed that Reese had ratted me out again.

"Well, it's kind of a love story," I suggested.

"What kind of a love story?"

"A monstery love story."

That didn't go over too well. She gave me that Mom look — you know the one — and I caved.

"Okay, okay, it's a monster story. And they don't love each other, they hate each other. But they put aside their differences and stomp the Earth into nothingness."

I left out the part about the cool explosions and the special effects.

"That is just the kind of movie that's going to rot your brain," she lectured. "You keep watching movies like that and you'll end up living in a trailer park and driving a used Hyundai."

"But Mom," I whined, "everyone's going to see it."

"And if everyone stuck their heads in the electric fan, would you want tickets to that, too?"

Is she kidding? Who wouldn't? At least to watch.

I tried to defend the movie on the grounds of freedom of expression, creativity, the rights of the filmmaker, and all kinds of stuff I got from a book. But what I got was a lot of head-shaking, several loud "No's," a "There's nothing you can do to change my mind," and a "That's final, little mister."

I'll take that as a huge maybe.

Being a parent must be tough, because you've always got to be ready to prevent your kids from having any fun. You're like the army. You're in a constant state of alert because as soon as a kid is having fun, you have to step in and stop it.

It doesn't matter if it's comic books, or cool movies, or music that's so loud I can't even hear the lyrics.

I think that's because when you're a parent, you're not having any fun. Your life is all about keeping house, going to work, fixing the car, taking care of kids, and worrying about money. Heck, the only fun they have is stopping _us_ from having fun.

And so parents get their revenge. They try to make us eat gross vegetables, watch movies with stupid singing in them, or block all the neat cable channels on the TV.

That's why it's important to see movies like <u>Predatory Aliens 6</u>. Because your mom doesn't want you to.

CHAPTER FOUR

"**P**lay with me."

I pretended not to hear. I sat at the kitchen table and worked on some stupid equations that are guaranteed not to come in handy later in life, unless I'm living on a space station.

"Malcolm?"

Still ignoring, I took the square root of one number, factored the result against another, multiplied by pi, and got a plastic ball shoved in my face.

"Play with me," Dewey said. "And Mr. Bounce."

Dewey stood in front of me holding a striped beach ball. He looked so wide-eyed and innocent that I did what any older brother would do.

"Get lost, Dewey," I replied. "Go bother someone else."

Dewey heard the *dingly-ding-ding* from the television and followed the music into the living room like a bee to fresh flowers. Reese was in his usual after-dinner spot — in the living room in front of the television. Dewey bounced Mr. Bounce to him.

I heard the ball pop. A piece of plastic flew past my head. Mr. Bounce was no more.

"Can't you see the TV's on?" Reese yelled at Dewey. "I'm watching cartoons!" Reese doesn't like to be disturbed when he's trying to figure out how they make cartoons move.

"How does Scooby do that?" he yelled. "I must've missed something!" I heard the distinctive sound of channel-surfing. He must've gone around the dial about twenty times before I heard the screams.

At first I thought Reese was watching wrestling or beating up on Dewey. It was better than that.

Much better.

"Car chase! Car chase! Car chase!" Reese yelled. Within seconds, we were all glued to the television. Police cars chased a beat-up SUV down the highway. There were sirens, flashing red lights, helicopters, the works!

We were like Romans at the Colosseum watching some crazy gladiator fighting lions. Only this time, the gladiator was an SUV and the lions had blue uniforms and helicopters.

"Look at the traction that SUV is getting," Dad observed. "I wonder what he's got under the hood."

Mom pulled out a notepad. She liked to keep track of the infractions. "Speeding, evading police officers, reckless endangerment . . ."

"He just ran a stop sign," Reese pointed out.

"That's three of those," Mom said.

Some families have game night or movie night or

something boring like that. One of the things that really brings my family together is a car chase on TV and the expectation of impending disaster. Only one of us wasn't watching the live broadcast. . . . Dewey.

"Will you play with me?" Dewey asked Dad. Dad shooed him away. Dewey tried Mom. No such luck. She gave him a gentle nudge.

"You're blocking the screen, honey," she said. "Hey, he's littering! That's a new one."

The SUV turned off the highway. We watched as the chase zigged and zagged down neighborhood streets.

"When can I get *my* license, Dad?" Reese asked.

"Long after I'm gone, son. Long after I'm gone."

We watched the SUV turn down our street. To heck with the TV, we ran to the window to watch it live! The SUV screeched to a stop in front of our house. We heard the helicopters flying overhead. Two fugitives, a man and a woman, jumped out and ran up our walkway.

"Hey, there are criminals in our yard," Reese pointed out. "And they're not Francis's friends."

"They're running up the porch!" I said. This was creepy and cool at the same time!

"Get down, boys," Dad said. "This is the part they don't always show on the news."

"Dewey!" Mom yelled. "Lock the front door."

And that's when the trouble started. Never send

Dewey to do a job that could easily be handled by a
one-armed monkey.

"Dewey!" Mom yelled again. Dewey moved to the
front door. But he didn't lock it. He opened it.

"Hi!" Dewey said to the fugitives. "Will you play
with me?"

CHAPTER FIVE

"**Q**uick! Out the back!" the man said. A woman followed as they ran through the living room to the kitchen and out the back door. Unfortunately, they ran right into the helicopter searchlight and saw several cops rushing through the backyard. It was just like that time Francis . . . well, let's just say we're not allowed to talk about *that* day anymore.

The fugitives slammed the door and locked it. They ran back to the living room. Dewey grabbed the man by the leg.

"What did you bring me, Santa?" he asked. "I've been good all year!"

The man shook Dewey off and looked around the living room. "Everybody sit down and be quiet," he said. "Don't open the door and don't answer the phone." He shoved his hand in his jacket. "Or else!"

I didn't need an IQ of 165 to figure out what was in his pocket.

"Oh, that's great, Don. Did you get that from a movie?"

"No, Delores. Video game. *Evil Resident III*."

"Well, what are we going to do now?" Delores asked. "This is *not* the big break in showbiz you promised me! We're a long way from Hollywood. And we're trapped with Mr. and Mrs. Family." She pointed to my parents.

Don thought for a minute. He rubbed his chin. He looked up at the ceiling. He looked at his shoes like he'd never seen them before. I've seen that look on Reese when he's trying to figure out how the salt stays on potato chips.

"You're wrong, Delores, my dear. We're trapped with Mr. and Mrs. Hostage and the entire Hostage family." He smiled.

"Are you one of Santa's helpers?" Dewey asked Delores.

Don and Delores didn't really look like criminals. They looked like high school dropouts on their way to the unemployment line. Oh, he had a cool denim jacket and short black hair, but he was kind of skinny. My guess is he's really old, almost 20. He was trying to grow a beard, but it just made his chin look dirty.

Delores had long blond hair and a perky little smile. She looked more like a cheerleader or a homecoming queen than a fugitive.

"You in the house! This is the police!" Wow. Those are eight words you don't want to hear yelled over a bullhorn on a Friday night. Unless you live across the street, of course.

"What do you want?" Don yelled from the window. "Leave us alone! We haven't done anything!"

I could show them Mom's checklist, but what would that prove?

While Don and Delores were talking to the police, Dad herded us into a corner with Mom. He had a plan. Dad loves adventure and excitement, but he just takes things a bit too far. Like the time he built a robot and filled it full of bees. Or the time he taught me to roller-skate and . . . well, the less said about *that* the better.

"When I give the signal, your mother will say the magic words. While those two criminals are distracted, we'll rush the front door and get out of here. Stay low, and if they get in your way, knock them down."

"Then can we kick them?" Reese asked.

"Only if there's time, son," Dad replied.

"Hal! What about the house?" Mom asked.

"That's why we have insurance, honey. It got us the automatic garage door last summer, didn't it?" He turned to us. "We go on three. One, two . . ."

"Three!" Dewey said.

"Grease fire!" Mom yelled.

Reese grabbed me and Dewey and shoved us into the kitchen. "Fire? Let's go!" he said.

I smacked him in the head. "There's no fire! That was the signal." He looked at me like a wounded animal. "The *magic* words," I said.

"No fire?" He was really disappointed.

It was too late now. Mom and Dad were out the

23

front door. Don jumped in front of it and blocked our exit.

"Quick! The back door!" I shoved Reese ahead of me.

"Quit shoving!" Reese shoved me back. I couldn't let him get away with that, could I? So I shoved him again. Then Dewey shoved me.

Before I knew it, Reese had me in a headlock. I was trying to stomp his feet, but Dewey had wrapped himself around my legs. We crashed to the floor like Stone Cold Steve Austin vs. The Rock vs. Goldberg.

"Ow! Cut it out!" the three of us yelled at the same time.

"Break it up!" Don yelled, just as I was about to bite Reese on the leg. Don was not a happy criminal. How could he be — he'd just lost forty percent of his hostages and all he had left was me, Reese, and Dewey.

"You just let Mr. and Mrs. Hostage escape," he yelled to Delores. "You were supposed to watch them! That's your job!"

"I'm an actress. You're supposed to get me to Hollywood!" she countered.

Reese tugged at my arm. "This is so cool," he whispered. "This guy Don has style. He got Mom and Dad out of the house and he got more cops on our front yard than Francis ever did. He's a rebel!"

Oh no. I saw the sparkle in Reese's eye. I knew

where this was going and there was nothing I could do to stop it.

"Excuse me." Reese tapped Don on his shoulder. "We've never had any celebrities in the house before. Can I have your autographs?"

This will only end in tears. Probably mine.

I'm stuck in the house with two lunatic adults. In other words, it's just another day in my life. Outside, the house was surrounded by cops, television cameras, neighbors, reporters . . . and Mom and Dad.

And I'm in here with my brothers and two criminals who can't tie their shoes or figure out the VCR.

But the thing that really bothers me? Why do these things always happen on weekends? There are five other days when I'm stuck in school, working on complex math problems, trying to figure out a way to avoid a Politically Correct History Quiz, and wondering if Kelly Craven really likes me.

Why can't chaos strike then? I mean, Monday through Friday, five days out of seven, you'd think the odds would be pretty much in my favor, right? Wrong. The odds always favor school.

Look at the great disasters through-
out history, the volcano that de-
stroyed Pompeii, the Titanic, the
sinking of Atlantis. I bet they all happened on weekends.

CHAPTER SIX

"**F**our pretty ladies," Francis said as he put the queens down on the table. "Read 'em and weep, boys." Francis was in the TV room at Marlin Academy, beating the other cadets at cards. He scooped up his winnings and shoved them into his pocket. "Nice playing with you."

Francis is the master of semi-legal games like pool, poker, and sports betting. He isn't just my older brother, he's my better brother. It's unfortunate that the growing pains of youth got him sent away to military school. With his blond hair and piercing eyes, he could easily be a model. Maybe not a role model, but a cool model? I can't believe how lucky I am to be related to him.

"That's it, Francis, I'm out of the game," Eric said. "I guess I'll get ready for tomorrow's ten-mile hike. You?"

"Haven't thought of my excuse yet," Francis replied. "But make no mistake — I'm not hiking ten miles or ten feet with a full backpack tomorrow at dawn. Or at noon. Or in the evening."

"Hey, Francis, I think you should see this." It was Joe. He was watching television. He had left the game earlier when he ran out of I.O.U's and family heirlooms.

Francis saw the news coverage starring Don, Delores, and our house. His mouth fell open.

"I didn't know your parents were having a party," Joe said.

"That doesn't look like a party," Eric said. "It looks like a riot."

Francis stared at the television. He didn't move or say anything.

"Don't worry, Francis," Eric consoled. "I'm sure they'll be all right. The police know what they're doing."

"Gentlemen," Francis said happily, "have fun on the hike. You'll be marching through mud and mosquito-filled swamps and I'll be enjoying one of my mom's home-cooked meals. I can practically taste the reheated canned chili now."

"What are you talking about?" Eric asked.

Francis pointed to the TV and smiled. "I've got a ticket home."

Francis picked up the phone. When the phone rang at our house. I reached for it.

"Stop!" Don yelled. My hand froze like a snowman in Siberia. Don reached in front of me and grabbed the phone.

"Who are you? What do you want?" he grilled the caller.

"Hello, this is officer Francis Olaf of the FBI," Francis bluffed into the phone. "Before we can do anything for you, I need some assurances that the hostages are all right."

"You can talk to Malcolm." Don said, handing me the phone. "Say hello, and remember," he patted his jacket pocket, "I'll be listening to every word."

"Is it Superman?" Dewey asked.

"Hello, young master Malcolm," the voice said from the phone as I shushed Dewey. "Don't say anything. Just listen. I have a plan."

"It's not 'run out the front door,' is it?" I whispered. "We already tried that and we lost Mom and Dad."

"I want you to hang in there, little brother. Play along with the criminals and don't do anything crazy unless you can find someone else to blame. I'll be there as quickly as I can."

That didn't sound like much of a plan, but the best part of it? Francis is coming home! I wonder if he wants a ticket to the movie?

CHAPTER SEVEN

"**S**ir? It's imperative that I be given an emergency leave of absence."

Nope. Almost. Too much inflection. Try again.

"Sir? Have you seen CNN today?"

No. Not urgent enough.

"Sir. My family is being held hostage."

Francis stood in the mirror practicing his lines. He needed to get just the right blend of urgency and despair in his voice. Oh, and tears. Tears were *always* good.

He had spent the last half hour in his room making sure that his Academy uniform was inspection-ready. It was cleaned and pressed, the creases were in their proper places, and his shoes were so shiny he could see his face. He wanted Commandant Spangler to focus on just the crisis and not the flaws in Francis' clothing.

Francis left his room and walked across the parking lot to Spangler's office. He knocked on the door.

"Come in, cadet," Spangler said. As always, Spangler was dressed in his military uniform. His bald head was shiny atop his tall frame. Even the eyepatch over his right eye looked orderly and precise.

He was shining his shoes with a motorized polishing attachment on the hook on his left arm.

"Sir? There's a personal emergency at home," Francis started.

"An emergency? Son, life is nothing but one emergency after another. From Bunker Hill to Pearl Harbor, from tax day to the day the Grim Reaper pays his first and final call."

Francis tried to interrupt, but he couldn't. Spangler wasn't pausing for breath.

"It's important that as we go through life, Cadet, we take what it throws at us and wrestle it to the ground. Hardship, then survival. That's what it's all about."

"Sir," Francis finally jumped in. "My family is being held hostage —"

"Cutthroats? Brigands? Communist spies? Cadet this is unspeakable. Why didn't you say something sooner?" Spangler stood up from his chair. "Let's mobilize the troops!"

Apparently Francis was going to have some company on his trip home.

CHAPTER EiGHT

"**O**kay. This is me," I said, taking one of Dewey's rare army men that didn't have his head chewed off and placing it in the middle of the house map I had drawn. "And this is you," I added, placing a pickle next to it.

"How come I'm the pickle?" Reese asked.

"Well, you could be a G.I. Joe torso," I replied.

"He's not so tough without his legs," Reese laughed and plopped the amputated doll next to the army man.

We were sitting on the floor of my bedroom. I was explaining my escape plan to Reese and Dewey. The way it was going so far, I might as well have been talking to . . . well, Reese and Dewey.

"Okay, so the pickle is Don and Delores," I said.

"Huh-huh," Reese chuckled. "They're a pickle."

"I want to be Domingo!" Dewey blurted and plopped his large, stinky teddy bear in the middle of my map.

"Dewey! Domingo's too big! He's crushing everything!"

Dewey pouted and lifted Domingo from the map. "Come on Domingo, we don't get to play house."

I pulled Domingo from Dewey's arms. "There!" I said. "You can be Domingo's ear." I tore the piece off Domingo's head and slapped it down next to the pickle.

The three of us huddled closer to the map like it was a warm fire on a cold day.

"I've been going over this and I think I've got everything figured out," I began.

"Good," Reese replied.

"The first thing we need to do is create some kind of diversion to get Don and Delores into the kitchen."

"Into the kitchen. Right."

"I don't know how. Explode something in the microwave, maybe. Then we head back here."

"Explosions? You have the best plans," Reese said.

"Are we gonna fly?" Dewey asked.

"I jimmied the bedroom window open," I said, ignoring Dewey. "We can climb out that way."

"Why would we want to do that?" Reese asked.

"To escape," I said slowly, stretching the last word out so that Reese could fully understand what I was talking about. I mean, this plan should be simple enough for a monkey to follow — but then, when has Reese ever been *that* smart?

"Escape!?" Reese exploded and stood away from the map. "Why would we want to do that?"

"Only two kinds of people want to escape: hostages and prisoners and in case you haven't been watching the live reports on channel 22, we definitely fall under the 'hostage' category!"

"Dude, look around!" Reese countered. "We've eaten nothing but junk food, we've watched a ton of great TV, didn't do our homework, have no parental supervision, no one's yelling at us, and as long as we don't let the police in the house or answer the phone, we can do pretty much anything we want! Why in the world would we ever want to escape this?" Reese stopped for a moment. He covered his heart and choked back a tear. "It's . . . paradise."

I didn't think the day would ever come without some type of severe tampering by medical science, but Reese had run circles around me logically. I thought I would be bailing him out of prison long before this word ever passed my lips, but Reese was *right*. Yeah, I had tickets to *Predatory Aliens 6*, but a total lack of parental supervision scores really high on the "Thing to Never Give Up" scale.

"I don't know, Reese. I mean these guys are criminals. There's a reason all those police cars are sitting out in front of the house trying to get these two to give themselves up."

"Yeah, they're trying to ruin my fun," Reese quipped.

I pointed out, "At any minute, the police could blast tear gas through the window. You realize that don't you?"

Reese's eyes widened. "You think? Oh man! Would *that* be cool or what?"

I gotta admit, it would be pretty cool. Sure my eyes would sting like someone set them on fire, but getting tear-gassed by the police would be pretty awesome. It'd definitely help my popularity at school.

But no matter what Reese thought, I just knew that staying a hostage was *not* a good idea. If it was, everyone would be doing it. This was going to end badly and I wanted to be far away when it did — preferably in a darkened theater watching people get devoured by hungry aliens.

And when I say this was going to end badly, I'm not talking about what's going to happen when the police finally catch Don and Delores. I'm talking about what'll happen when Mom does.

Don came into the room and looked down at the army man, the G.I. Joe torso and the pickle. "What're you up to?" he asked.

"Malcolm's planning an escape," Reese quickly confessed. "But don't worry. I'll put a stop to anything he tries. I'm riding this horse until it drops."

I don't believe it! Sold out by my own brother without so much as a bribe. At least he could've squeezed out five bucks first. Reese wanted to stay and now that Don was given the 411 on my plan, there was no chance of me ending this stupid thing.

"Escape, huh?" Don looked at my layout. He reached down, snatched the pickle slice and flicked it into his mouth. "That'll be pretty hard to do without the pickle." He gave a few satisfied chews and left the room.

Reese doubled-over with laughter.

"What? What?" I asked, irritated that he'd ratted me out.

"He just ate Delores."

CHAPTER NINE

"**W**hat are you doing to get my precious children out of there? I didn't go through hours of painful labor just to give birth to hostages!"

Mom was screaming at Chief of Police Klemp, the man in charge. Klemp looked big and tough, like a guy who could eat cars for a hobby.

I'm pretty sure Mom could take him. I'm sure she thought so, too.

"Why are you just standing around?" she insisted.

"There is a process to this, ma'am," Chief Klemp said as he leaned against his car, arms folded. "You remember that time with Francis."

"We don't talk about that," Mom said.

"This is all very by-the-book," Chief Klemp continued.

Then he started to recite the book. "First we wait for things to settle down. Surround the house. Alert the neighbors. Get the news people in position. That way nobody does anything foolish."

"What then?" Dad asked.

"Then we open up a dialogue," Chief Klemp replied. "Get them talking. Find out what they want.

Once we have their list of demands, we move forward into the negotiating phase."

"Negotiate? What's to negotiate?" Mom said. I don't think she'd ever heard the word before. Mom knows lots of words that end in "-ate." "Dictate" is one of her personal favorites.

"Everything's negotiable. The FBI's sending over a hostage negotiator. And we're waiting for him. So I suggest you just be patient."

"Why?"

That was when Chief Klemp uttered the words I thought I'd never hear anyone ever say to Mom. "Because I said so."

Wow. Is that awesome or what?

Mom was speechless, but only for a moment. "What happens when they don't want to negotiate?"

"Then we cut off the electricity, the SWAT team rushes the place, and we wait for the smoke to clear," Chief Klemp said. "Right now, we're in the 'Don't Do Anything Foolish' phase." The Chief massaged his nightstick and eyed our house. "I know. It's not my favorite, either."

Mom grabbed Dad and stomped away. She pushed past the barricade and stormed up the sidewalk to the front door. She knocked. And knocked.

Dewey and I went for the door, but Don stopped us. What he couldn't stop was Reese, who was coming down the hallway. Reese opened the door and saw Mom and Dad.

"Reese, I want to talk to the criminals. I can straighten this out in five minutes."

Reese thought for a minute. I could tell he was thinking. He almost fainted from the pressure. Stay in the house with criminals. Let Mom and Dad in. He slammed the door. Then he smiled the biggest smile I've ever seen on his face.

"Reese! You open this door right now, mister!" she yelled.

"I can't," Reese replied. He was practically convulsed with laughter. "Malcolm won't let me."

CHAPTER TEN

"The way I see it, our parents are gone. Maybe forever."

That's Reese. The guy who just slammed the door on Mom and Dad. They sent Francis to military school for behavior like that.

"Did they go to Mars?"

That's Dewey. What can you say to that?

We sat at the kitchen table because Reese had promised us an important announcement. Maybe he had an escape plan. I'd been racking my brain but it was a tough equation. The doors are locked. Cops are on the outside. Criminals are on the inside, threatening us with a lot of "or elses."

And I used to think biology was tough.

"We're on our own," Reese declared. "And we've got to face reality."

"Whose reality?" I asked.

"From this moment forward, we have no parents," Reese announced. "We're orphans. That means candy for breakfast, no more school, and no more chores. Anarchy rules."

"Yippee!" Dewey said.

"That's just crazy talk, Reese," I said. "Our parents are right outside that door, and sooner or later, they'll be coming back in."

Reese kept going. "Well until they return, if that ever happens, I'm in charge."

"What? No way," I protested.

"I'm the oldest, the numero uncle."

"It's numero uno," I corrected.

"Exactly. I'm the new man of the house."

"And I'll be the mommy," Dewey said.

There's no way Reese is going to be in charge of the house. No way. First, it's totally wrong. You don't put the lunatics in charge of the asylum, and you don't put Reese in charge of anything. Dewey can be the mommy, though.

"Let's put it to a vote," I suggested.

Reese put up his hand. "I vote for me."

I put up my hand. "And I vote for me."

We both looked at Dewey. "It's up to you, Dewey," Reese said. "If you vote for me, I promise not to hit you for almost eight whole minutes."

"You're the tiebreaker." I winked at him.

Dewey waited, like, forever, before speaking. And when he finally spoke, I wished he hadn't.

"I vote for . . . chocolate," he said and pulled out a candy bar and shoved it in his mouth.

"That settles it. I'm the man of the house," Reese announced.

"No, I'm the man of the house," Don said as he entered the kitchen. "And what is there to eat in my house?" Don started opening cabinets.

"Okay," Reese whispered. "He's number one. But I'm number two."

Sometimes he has no idea what he's saying.

CHAPTER ELEVEN

"**A**re you from outer space?" Dewey asked. "Why are Martians called Martians? I have ten toes. How many do you have?"

"Well, Dewey," she said, "I have —"

"Are you my new mother? My old mother always gave me five dollars."

Dewey was being Dewey again. Irritating. At least his questions were directed at Delores.

"Do sea horses eat sea hay? How many grapes are in a grapefruit?" Dewey kept going. He had more questions than a college entrance exam.

On the sofa, Reese, Don, and me watched my house on television. That's right. Watched my house. On television. It's worse than golf.

No cartoons, no wrestling, no talk shows. Nothing good like that. We could only watch news programs that broadcast live from my front yard.

"Boring," I complained. "There's no fighting, no yelling, no chair-throwing. This isn't television."

"This is news," Don explained. "*My* news."

"And maybe the house will blow up," Reese said.

Delores stomped over to the television and stood in front of it. "They're just showing the house. How is this going to launch our careers in Hollywood if no one gets a good look at us?"

"I'm working on it, honey. Genius takes time."

And that's what it's been like for the last half hour. Don and Delores argue, Dewey irritates Delores, and Reese watches television. And I'm counting down the hours until my movie starts.

I excused myself and went to the bathroom. When I looked up through the window, I saw Mom's face! Okay, that's going to leave a scar!

"Open the window," she yelled through the glass. "We're getting you out of there now!" Behind her, Dad gave a little wave.

"Do what your mother says, son," he said.

I unlocked the window and gave a shove. Nothing. I pushed harder. Still nothing. Then I remembered. Mom and Dad had the window nailed shut to keep Francis from sneaking out. There was nothing I could do except shrug, close the curtains and do what I came to do.

When I came back to the living room, Don and Delores were still arguing, but now a reporter was on the TV.

"We're live now at the front yard where a hostage crisis is threatening the neighborhood and everyone is asking the same question: Who are these people? Where did they come from and what do they want? We'll have more on this story as it develops. I'm Allan Barnhart from Triple Action News. Triple the action, triple the news."

"Who does he *think* we are?" Don yelled at the television as if it was going to answer. "I'm Don Lindstrom and this is Delores Manville! She's one of the great undiscovered actresses of all time and I'm her manager. What more could you want?"

I couldn't take it anymore. Even though Mom and Dad were out of the house, there was so much yelling it was like having Mom and Dad back in the house. I had to do something because if things didn't start happening, I might not get to my movie.

"Look," I began, "you both have an opportunity here. A once-in-a-lifetime shot. This is great publicity. Why not talk to the reporter?"

Don and Delores looked confused. But since nobody said "Shut up, kid," I kept going.

"Invite that guy inside. Let him get to know you as people. Set the record straight. Let him hear the legend of Don Lindstrom and Delores Manville."

"Delores and Don," Delores corrected.

"Whatever . . . as long as it's Don and Delores," Don also corrected.

"How would you like a job as our publicity manager, kid?" he asked.

I'd hate it. But it has to be better than watching my house on TV.

Most kids have their first job and it's a very simple one. Paper route, mowing lawns, baby-sitting. Those are safe, sane jobs for kids. You can make some extra money, not work too hard and everything's okay.

Some kids are born rich. They never have to worry about working. They get cool cars, great clothes, a personal chef to make all their food for them.

Then there's me. I get hand-me-down clothes from Reese, when I mow the lawn it's called a chore, and I have to make my own peanut-butter-and-banana sandwiches.

And years from now, maybe when I'm interviewing for college, people will ask me about my interests and activities and work experience.

I can't lie. I'll have to tell them the truth. "I was the official spokesperson for some criminals that had taken my family hostage."

No matter what my SAT scores or grade point average indicates, that's just not going to sound good.

CHAPTER TWELVE

"**W**ere you really a bully in school?" Reese asked Don. "What was your favorite bank to rob? How many times have you been on *America's Most Wanted*? How many speeding tickets do you have? Who's your favorite criminal?"

Reese had nearly as many questions as Dewey. It's always nice to see Reese take an interest in something.

I had negotiated with the reporter Allan Barnhart for an exclusive thirty-minute interview with Don and Delores.

But as soon as Mr. Barnhart sat down and turned the camera on, Reese squeezed between Don and Delores and started asking Don his own questions.

Not for long, though. As soon as Reese paused for breath, Don picked him up and locked him in the bathroom.

"Is this part of your training program?" Reese asked from behind the bathroom door. "Hey, is that gum?"

Don't ask. You don't want to know.

The reporter turned his attention to Don and Delores. "Why are you doing this?" he asked.

"Just a minute," I said. "We have a list of questions that you can ask." I tore out a sheet of paper from my school notebook. Don and I had each come up with a list of questions. Mr. Barnhart started with Don's. There were questions that Don thought would really help people to understand him.

Y'know, in many ways, he makes Dewey seem like a Nobel Prize winner.

He scanned it then looked at me. "What if it's not on the list?"

Don and Delores looked at me. I nodded. "Then, we don't answer."

"Right," Don agreed.

Delores combed her hair. Don tucked in his shirt. The cameras were turned on and we got the preliminary questions out of the way.

"Favorite color?" Mr. Barnhart asked.

"Red. No, wait, green. Blue!" Don said. "That's it, midnight blue. I'm sure of it."

"Favorite food?" Mr. Barnhart sighed.

"Beets. No, wait. Herring. No, I've got it — dill pickles."

"Maybe we should move on to *Malcolm's* questions now," Delores suggested. Mr. Barnhart looked relieved as he flipped to the next page.

He asked the first question, "How did all of this start?" It was like he'd hit the "on" button. Delores went first.

"Okay, first off, I did not steal that car. I only borrowed it from my ex-boyfriend. He offered to loan it to me once. Yeah, I know that was before we broke up, but he did offer, right? And that's what really started all this trouble. I just needed a way to get to Hollywood to be a star."

"Tell him about the award," Don urged.

"Oh, right. I was voted Miss Superstructure by the local Home Builder's Association," she said proudly.

"That looks good on any résumé," Don boasted. "That's why I'm going to be her manager, and her producer, and her agent. I have a natural ability with money and creative people."

"Those bounced checks were the bank's fault, not Don's," Delores continued. "And he wouldn't have gotten fired from the Shop 'Til You Drop market except for a personality conflict with the customers and some missing cash that probably wasn't his fault. At least not all of it."

Don added, "I didn't hold up that liquor store either. I was looking at certain items and they ended up shoved into my jacket. Is it my fault that the clerk panicked? He was the one who started throwing money at me. We never heard the sirens, either. That car has a killer sound system and we were totally rockin'!"

"And singing along," Delores offered.

"And I didn't even see the police cars until we ran out of gas in front of the kid's house."

Delores added, "He's right. His eyes are really bad. He's been saving for an eye exam and that phaser surgery."

"Phaser" surgery? Why? So he can see *Star Trek* better from a distance?

Reese sat down beside me, his greasy hands holding the bathroom door hinges and a screwdriver. He elbowed me, grinning. "Hear this? These excuses are a gold mine," he whispered. "Eye exam! That's a keeper!"

Oh, no. Reese taking his inspiration from criminals? The only good thing is that Reese has the memory capacity of an action figure. Francis can't get here too soon.

Then Delores looked right at the camera and said, "My going to Hollywood was a dream of my grandmother's before she departed."

"I'm sorry," Mr. Barnhart said. "What did she die from?"

"She didn't die. She just departed. She was behind in the rent on our trailer home."

"See?" Don said. "We're just a couple of hardworking Americans trying to live the American dream of freedom, the pursuit of happiness and the fame that comes from being famous. We're going to make it big in show business."

"And modeling," Delores added.

"Movies. Don't forget movies."

"And female mud wrestling."

"That's right," Don said. "No one can body slam like my Delores."

In less time than it takes to make a crank call, Delores had reached over and looped her right arm around Don's left arm. With one little tug, she flipped him over her back and slammed him to the floor.

"I taught her that," Don said proudly as he lay on the rug. Wow. Maybe she could teach *me* that.

"Will this be on the news tonight?" Delores asked Mr. Barnhart. "I'd like to call some of my friends."

"I'm not sure," the reporter responded. "There was a lawn mower fire on Draper Road and Farmer Brown claims to have the world's largest pimento."

Don pulled out his wallet and snapped out a crisp five-dollar bill. He handed it to the reporter. "How about now?" he said conspiratorially.

"You could take your lady out to a fine dinner," Delores suggested. She's right. Especially if they go to Burger Barn.

The reporter carefully folded the bill and put it in his pocket. "I'd say things are looking in your favor."

CHAPTER THIRTEEN

"Look sharp, cadets," Spangler said. "This is D day, the call to action. This will separate the men from the boys. It's what many of us have waited for our entire lives."

The cadets were dressed in their uniforms, each with a full backpack. Spangler had mobilized his troops. Within minutes of his order, they had marched from their rooms, across the grounds to his office.

"At ease, men," Spangler said.

Spangler sat watching the phone. He had called the governor to let her know Marlin Academy was on alert and ready to move across state lines should they be needed.

"This is ridiculous," Francis whispered. "It's time for action." He turned to Commandant Spangler. "Sir, I'd like to take a small contingent with me to monitor the perimeter for incoming messages."

Spangler didn't take his eyes off the phone and waved Francis off. Francis took this as the equivalent of "okay" and left the room with cadets Eric, Finley, and Joe.

Francis pulled out a piece of paper featuring a hand-drawn map of our house and the surrounding neighborhood. "This is ground zero," he said. "My parent's house." He pointed to the little square.

"Your parents live in a box?" Eric said.

"No, that's a representation."

"Maybe you should use drafting tools," Eric said. "This is way too abstract."

Ten minutes later, Francis and the three cadets had retreated to a classroom with all sorts of drafting equipment. Francis drew an accurate map of the neighborhood, probably because he had a lot of experience eluding capture while running through it.

"Now this is the Davis place," Francis said. "And over here is the Gleusteens, then the Guilfords."

"What's this empty lot?" Joe asked.

"Oh, uh, that's where the Larson house burned down." They all looked at Francis. "Don't look at me that way. Who knew that mail-order fireworks couldn't be trusted?"

Francis gave them his plan. They were now a secret unit of the Francis Rescue Team. Their first job was to get out of Marlin Academy and make their way to Francis's house to rescue us from the clutches of Don and Delores.

"And after that?" Eric said.

"Vegas," Francis said. "There's a lot of work to be done in Vegas. Now, how much cash does each of you have?"

CHAPTER FOURTEEN

"**T**his is just typical of that family," Mrs. Davis said. "Here it is the middle of the night, none of us can sleep, and why? Because *they've* been taken hostage."

Mrs. Davis and several other neighbors were being interviewed by Mr. Barnhart. Talking to the neighbors? There's a job I never want. That's worse than taking out the trash or trying to put Dewey to bed.

"Remember that time they dug up my lawn looking for China?" Mrs. Gleusteen said. "Not the country — the dishes they stole from me."

Everyone nodded in agreement.

"Or brought those llamas home from the zoo?" Mrs. Davis offered. "They spit on my dear Walter."

Walter is her shi-tzu, the kind of dog that looks like a mop. If any dog ever deserved spitting on, it was Walter.

"And I'm sure they're the ones causing the changes in the weather pattern," Mrs. Guilford said. "I just can't prove it. Yet."

That is so not true. We did free the llamas. They looked like half horse and half giraffe. Who knew you couldn't ride them? But we have nothing to do with the weather. *That* experiment totally failed. Besides, it was all Dabney's fault. He calibrated the satellite on his own.

"Wait just a minute!" Mom broke in. "You three are the biggest gossips in the neighborhood. With your backbiting and snippy little comments you've hurt more people than any of my kids."

Most people would be happy with that. They'd smile knowing that they had put their offenders in their place. But did that stop Mom?

What do you think?

She turned to Mrs. Guilford. "Isn't your husband stealing cans from *her* recycling bin?" She pointed to Mrs. Gleusteen. "And aren't you illegally connected to her cable system?" she said to Mrs. Davis. "And what's the deal with all those pet mice? Don't think we haven't noticed that, either."

Mrs. Guilford, Mrs. Davis, and Mrs. Gleusteen all looked at one another. It was more like a glare, really. An angry stare.

"Why you —" Mrs. Gleusteen shouted.

"I'll —" Mrs. Guilford yelled.

"That's the —" Mrs. Davis screamed.

"Smile, please." Flash! A photographer took a group picture. But only my mom was smiling. The other women pulled each other's hair and rolled around on the ground.

Now why aren't they showing *this* on TV!

CHAPTER FiFTEEN

"And just what do my taxes go for?" Mom had resumed her dialogue with Chief Klemp. Although it looked a lot like shouting. "Can you answer me that?" she asked. "Why won't anyone do something?" She poked at my dad. "Hal, say something."

But dad was busy looking under the hood of Don's SUV. "Honey," he said, "you should see the size of the engine they've got in this thing. Definitely a custom job."

Dad looked up and saw that Mom was giving him that "Are You Listening To Me?" stare. Dad got that look on his face. The one that said he'd better agree. I think that's the secret to a happy marriage. Agreeing with Mom.

"Y'know," he said, "I have to say that even Matlock would've had the boys out of there sooner." Then he ran his index finger over the engine block. "Wow. This baby's been steam-cleaned."

"Please, people, I understand your concerns," the understanding police chief said. "Believe me, I have kids of my own. Granted they've gone off to college and never call or write except to ask for money, but I love 'em just the same."

Mom was glaring at Chief Klemp so hard that I could almost see red-hot laser beams of anger bore into his brain.

"Okay!" Chief Klemp finally said. "We'll try one thing. But when that hostage negotiator from the FBI shows up, it's going to be all your fault!"

Klemp walked away to talk to one of his officers. They talked quietly for a moment.

"Francis isn't in there, is he?" Chief Klemp asked, turning back to my mom.

"No, he's still away at Marlin Academy."

"And a good place for him." He turned to the officer. "What did we use last time?"

"We had a similar situation a couple of years ago at Sam Francisco's Import World of Food. We tried the gas, but it spoiled all the produce. We're still fighting it out in court. But last month, we loaned the dogs to the Statesville City PD. They haven't given them back yet."

"Tear gas it is," Klemp decided. "Fire it up!" He turned to Mom. "Living room window?"

Mom pointed directly in front of her. "What are you doing?" she suddenly asked.

One of the policemen shouldered at tear gas gun.

"Wait a minute!" Mom yelled. "My kids are in there!" But it was too late.

Inside the living room, Don and Delores were having another argument, this one was about the best route to Hollywood. Delores wanted to follow the "cute little red lines" on the map. Don preferred the blue ones. I didn't have the heart to tell him those were state borders.

There was the sound of shattering glass, and then a metal canister bounced across the living room. Tear gas!

"Stink bomb!" Reese cried. He dove under the sofa cushions. "This is sooooo cool!"

"Don't look at me," Dewey said. "I haven't eaten since this morning."

Don and Delores jumped behind the TV. I hid behind a chair. The canister sparked and fizzled. Then a bunch of goo leaked out on the rug.

"Kid," Don yelled. "Go check it out."

"You check it out," I said. "I'm staying right here."

"I'm in charge, mister," Don replied. "And you'll do as I say."

Argh! Don was becoming more dadlike. I stared at the canister on the living room floor. Usually, these things emit gas that's supposed to make us cry and race out the front door. This one just lay there like a metal lump. I poked it with a pencil and rolled it over. On the bottom was a little sticker. "Best if used before November 1994."

I guess there wasn't much use for tear gas in town. Reese ran out from behind the sofa and grabbed the canister. Holding it in front of him, he chased Dewey around the living room.

"Look out! It's going to explode! The house is going to blow up!"

"Aaaahhh! Get away from me, smoke monster!" Dewey cried.

CHAPTER SIXTEEN

"**R**ight on time," the train conductor said as he looked at his watch. "Only 48 minutes late."

The conductor stood in front of Francis, Finley, Eric, and Joe. "You boys can catch the bus right over there at the terminal."

The top secret Francis Rescue Team exited the train. Francis stopped at the bottom of the stairs. He stared at the train, then looked at his ticket. Then he looked at the bus terminal and then at Finley.

"Oh, Finley," Francis started, "Why are we here?"

"That's where the tickets are for, Francis," Finley replied.

"But I don't live here. My family isn't being held hostage here."

"Missouri," said Joe helpfully.

"You were in charge of transportation, Finley," Francis said. "You are the travel coordinator for the Francis Rescue Team."

Francis was not happy. Finley was just a little bit nervous.

"I hear it's a nice town," he said. "It offers a wealth of history and traditional Southern architecture. It gets three stars in the Triple-A guidebook."

"Uh, huh. And —" Francis waited for the real reason.

Finley finally let out the truth. "This is the first time I've been out of Marlin in over six months. I thought we could swing around and say hello to my mother first. She hasn't been feeling too well lately, and I just —"

"You idiot," Eric exploded. "Why would you think we wanted to see your mother first? What's *that* all about?"

"Gentlemen, please," Francis calmed. "We could argue like this all afternoon, but it won't solve our basic needs of food, shelter, transportation, and cash."

"Yeah. Right," Eric said. "We're stuck in the middle of nowhere and with what? Nothing. That's what."

"But we do have Finley's mother." Francis put his arm around Finley. "Tell me, Finley, is she a good cook?"

"The best, Francis. She makes a baklava that's so sweet it makes you cry. And her pork and beans taste as fresh as the day she opened the can."

"That's all I need to hear," Francis replied as they all walked toward the bus station. "By the way, Finley, how much cash does your mom keep on her?"

CHAPTER SEVENTEEN

In almost anyone's house, the most important thing in the kitchen is the refrigerator, 'cause that's where people keep food and stuff. But not our house. Our veggie crisper is empty; the only vegetables we have come in a colored sauce.

The most important thing in our kitchen is the can-opener. That one simple tool is the only way to eat. Without it, all those cans of beans, chili, Spaghetti-O's, soup, tuna, and pork weenies are worthless. Now that I think about it? Even with a can opener some of that crud is still worthless.

Don fired up the can opener. Its hum filled the house and Dewey and Reese raced to the kitchen like two of Pavlov's best dogs.

"Oh boy!" Reese enthused. "Maybe he's opening the canned hash!"

"That's only for Sundays," I reminded my brother.

"He doesn't know that!" Reese said excitedly, licking his lips.

"Is canned hash made of monkeys?" Dewey asked Delores.

"No sweetheart, it's made of —"

"What plant makes cheese?"

"Sweetheart, cheese doesn't —"

"If flies fly, why don't birds bird?"

Delores's fingers began to twitch. She slowly backed out of the room, never taking her eyes off Dewey, just in case he followed.

Don opened the can of corned beef hash and put it into the microwave.

"Shouldn't you pour that into a bowl, first?" I asked.

"If you wanna eat fancy-like, I suppose," Don returned.

This was not going well. Eating mom's food was like playing Las Vegas roulette. You spun the wheel, took your chances, and hoped that whatever substance she was passing off as dinner wouldn't make you too sick or give Dewey gas.

What am I saying? Breathing gives Dewey gas.

Mom was an expert at cooking with these processed, chemical-ridden foods. Mix the wrong ingredients and I swear the house could explode. Or maybe your intestines. In Don's hands, this was going to be a nightmare — but not mine.

I mean, being a genius and all, genius-type ideas often come to me. Okay, maybe they weren't *always* genius ideas, but most of them involved fun without fire. But this one . . . this idea was worthy of . . . of . . . I don't know, someone *really* smart.

"I've got an idea," I offered.

Reese grabbed my shirt and tugged me closer. "Shut up!" he hissed. "You'll ruin this for all of us! Don opened the canned hash *and* the sardines!"

65

I peeled Reese's fingers from my T-shirt. "Why don't you order pizza?"

Before the words left my mouth, Reese nearly fainted.

"P-pizza?" he whimpered. "I never thought . . . I never imagined we could . . ." Choked with emotion, Reese grabbed me and hugged me like I had just handed him a hundred dollar bill. "You are a genius," I heard his muffled voice say, buried in my shoulder.

Don looked at the corned beef hash and sardine cans. "Who's gonna pay for it?" he asked.

"I knew it was too good to be true!" Reese moaned.

"Just have the cops pay," I suggested.

Reese's and Don's faces both lit up like Christmas trees. Reese leaped from the table, grabbed the two open cans from the microwave and raced out of the kitchen.

"Where're you going?" I called after him.

"I'm hiding these under my bed! I'll eat like a king all week!"

It was time to execute Stage Two of my plan. "Of course, I'm sure that once the police pay for the pizza, they'll want to trade a hostage for it."

"What? Where am I going to get a hostage to trade for food?" Don bemoaned. "Dang it! Reese! Bring back that canned hash!"

This guy may never make the Ten Most Wanted list, but he was making a solid bid for the Ten Most Boneheaded.

"Don! Don! You can trade *me* for the pizza," I suggested eagerly.

"You'd do that for me and Delores?" Don said, growing emotional.

To get out of this house? I'd trade myself for a pizza. I'd even eat one that Mom made. Of course, doing that would get me out of the house and into an ambulance.

Don and I headed to the living room where Delores sat in a chair with Dewey in her lap. Her eyes were closed and her nails dug into the chair's armrest.

"Would it hurt if I poked this into your nose?" Dewey asked her.

"Now that wouldn't be a very nice thing to — ouch!"

"Honey!" Don enthused. "We're getting pizza with the king o' toppings, baby! And all we gotta do is trade the cops this kid."

"I don't want to go," I lied. "But I'll do what's best for you and Don."

"Is pizza made of monkeys?" Dewey asked Delores.

Delores shot up from the chair. "No! Pizza is not made of monkeys! Canned hash is not made of monkeys! Only *monkeys* are made of monkeys!" she shouted.

Delores looked at Don. Tears welled in her eyes. This was not a good thing. I grabbed Don's hand.

"Come on!" I pushed. "Time to trade me for that pizza! Right! Me? Pizza? Right?"

Wrong.

So what lesson did I learn here? Sometimes it's better to be irritating than smart. I mean, when there are people trapped somewhere and only one of them can leave, they never say "send the smart one"!

No. They always send the irritating one or the smelly one. The smart one always has to stay behind to work on a backup plan to save everyone else's butt.

That's why, if I'm, like, ever in a disaster or something, when they look around for someone to solve all the problems, I'm not going to say a word. I'm just going to run around and throw bananas at people. The rescue ship will come and all the people who are tired of being hit by bananas will say "Take that guy first." And off I'll go.

Sounds crazy? Think it'll never work? Well if I had spent my time throwing bananas at Don and Delores instead of plotting to get pizzas, guess who'd be out with the police right now.

Yeah. Yeah. Yeah. It'd <u>still</u> be Dewey. He's irritating <u>and</u> smelly.

CHAPTER EiGHTEEN

"**D**o you know Batman?" Dewey asked the police officer.

The officer didn't answer, but snatched Dewey from Don's hands and left behind four boxes of cheese pizza with one topping. Or as Don had put it, "*the* topping."

Don picked up the pizza boxes and slowly backed into the house. "This better not be Little Caesar's!" he called out.

Mom and Dad watched the officer carry Dewey across the lawn and in the exact opposite direction of were they stood.

"Where are they taking him?" Mom asked.

"Interrogation," Chief Klemp answered.

"Interro — he's a child!"

"A child who knows every room inside that house," Chief Klemp responded.

"*We* know every room inside that house!"

"And when the FBI gets here, you can tell them all about it," Chief Klemp offered.

"You're not gonna . . . put bamboo shoots under his fingernails, are you?" Dad asked, concerned about Dewey.

"No sir," Chief Klemp stated. "We only do that to prisoners. Now excuse me. It's interrogation time."

Chief Klemp disappeared into the command tent and sat in front of Dewey.

"Okay, son," Chief Klemp began. "I need you to tell me everything you remember about the crooks. Did they say anything about their plans, did they have guns, how did they behave? Anything, anything you tell us would be helpful."

Chief Klemp stared at Dewey, waiting for a response. He'd have better luck questioning a goldfish. Actually, now that I think about it? Goldfish are about a billion times more focused.

Finally, Dewey stopped chewing on his tongue and said, "Delores smells like candy."

"Okay, son. I didn't really mean that *anything* you tell us would be helpful. Only helpful things are helpful. Do you understand?"

"Do you like hot dogs?" Dewey asked.

"I prefer hambur — look, we need to get your brothers out of the house. You'd like that, wouldn't you?"

"No. Reese hits me."

"He won't hit you if you save him," Chief Klemp offered.

"Yes he will," Dewey returned.

"No. He won't."

"Yes. He. Will."

"Look! I say he won't so he won't!" Chief Klemp finally erupted. "Now please, son, please, tell me how many guns they have in there."

71

Silence again. That was pretty amazing: Dewey being silent twice in under five minutes. But with Dewey, you couldn't be sure if he was thinking about what Chief Klemp had said or if his brain was just working its way around to more stupid questions.

"Do you know Batman?" Dewey finally asked.

See.

"No. I don't know Batman," Chief Klemp said through gritted teeth. "Because Batman isn't real! He doesn't exist! He's a cartoon!"

Dewey was stunned. How could someone claim that Batman wasn't real?

"Batman's not real?" Dewey asked, sure he'd heard wrong.

"No!" Chief Klemp growled back.

"Then who's gonna stop The Joker?" Dewey cried out.

CHAPTER NINETEEN

Don plopped the pizzas on the table and cracked open the top box.

Reese snatched a piece of pizza and eyed it suspiciously. "Anchovies?!" He blurted out and turned to Don. "I must be in heaven."

"You and me both, kid," Don said, stuffing a piece in his mouth.

"Please, call me Reese. 'Kid' puts so much distance between us."

If the anchovies didn't make me sick, these two would. Luckily, my fish-fest was interrupted by a booming voice.

"Listen mister!" It was my mom shouting through a bullhorn outside.

Like she needed a bullhorn to be heard? My mom *was* a bullhorn. Especially when Reese and I play "Stick the Green Beans to Dewey's Forehead" at the dinner table.

Pfff. It's not like he doesn't *ask* us to.

"I'm only gonna say this once, Don! If you so much as even think about hurting one hair on my babies' heads, I swear that I will dedicate the rest of my life to hunting you down," she shouted into the bull-horn.

"Come on, give us back the bullhorn, lady," I heard a police officer say.

"No!"

"This isn't going to help," the officer said in a calm tone.

Calm tone? Like that'd ever work with Mom when she gets on a roll. Try a straitjacket and a hammer. Maybe then you'll have some luck. Maybe. How big is the hammer?

"Help? What do you know about help?" Mom spat back at the officer. "All of you are just sitting around, hiding behind your cars, and eating your dough-nuts!"

"We don't have any doughnuts," the officer replied. "That's just a hurtful stereotype."

"Yeah, but if you did, you'd be stuffing them down that food hole of yours!"

"Doughnuts?" Dad said, coming out of the police command center with a cup of coffee. "Did I hear someone say doughnuts?"

"Oh, Hal! Really! Our children are suffering and all you can think of is food," Mom shouted and stormed away.

"Honey, we have to let the proper authorities han-dle this," Dad said, not that Mom could hear.

"She's a handful," the officer told Dad and patted him on the back.

"And that's just how I like her." Dad turned to the

officer and smiled. "Now where are those dough-nuts?"

The officer looked around, making sure my mom wasn't lurking about, ready to pounce. "Over here," he whispered.

Meanwhile, we had just polished off the fourth pizza. And by "we" I mean Reese, Don, and Delores. After picking anchovies off two slices, my fingers reeked like a garbage can behind the Chips Ahoy! fish-and-chips restaurant.

"I'll be in the living room," I said and pushed my chair away from the table.

"Can I have your fish mountain?" Reese asked, pointing to the pile of anchovies that were sitting by my plate.

"Just don't throw them at me."

"Never mind," Reese said and went back to eating his pizza.

I wandered into the living room and plopped down in front of the TV.

Some say the computer is the greatest invention in mankind's history. Others think penicillin. But if you ask me, it's no contest. It's TV. Sure video games come close, but TV is always there for you. It's the friend who never sleeps, the parent who's never too busy for you, and the brother who never hits you. It makes you laugh. It makes you cry. It makes you buy things. It never tells you to clean your room or go to bed, but right now it was telling me "There's clean underwear in the dryer."

What?

Oh, no. Please. Not this. Not Mom.

This time she had wrestled a microphone from that reporter, Alan Barnhart, and now her face was filling my TV screen telling the world where my clean underwear was.

"Malcolm, this is your mother talking," she said into the microphone.

Duh. Even from the depths of my embarrassment I could still figure *that* one out.

"I just wanted you to know that we both love you very much, sweetie," she continued, gripping the microphone like her hand was a vise. "And Reese, too." Barnhart tried to pull the microphone away. Like, a monster truck couldn't drag that thing outta my mom's hand.

"Do your homework, sport," Dad said, leaning into the camera frame. He took a huge bite from a Bear Claw and chewed. "A hostage situation is no reason to fall behind in your studies." He chewed some more doughnut before adding "and don't forget to take out the garbage."

I never thought the day would come, but it did. Betrayed by TV. Maybe penicillin isn't all that bad.

Luckily, the nightmare finally ended when Barnhart ambushed my mom. The last thing I saw before the station went to a "please stand by" signal was my mom kicking Barnhart in the shins.

Parents just don't get it. Okay, I know that's like saying the sky is blue, but this is something I've actually lost sleep over. If you had a mom like mine, and for your sake I hope you don't, you'd lose sleep over this, too.

I mean, think about it: Do they understand the concept of embarrassment? Are they on some totally different planet where humiliation doesn't exist? Is there really a need to show the picture of me at age nine with the Jell-o mold stuck around my neck to everyone who knocks on our door?

There is nothing, and I mean nothing, worse you can do to a kid than to embarrass him. Take away TV. Ban video games. Forbid junk food. Go ahead! Those things are a stroll in the park compared to the daily terror of embarrassment.

And the worst part is, parents are

like embarrassment machines. Baby photos, "My child is an 'A' student" bumper stickers, knitted sweaters from Aunt I-Can't-Knit. The list goes on and on.

I know this much: When I become a parent, I'm going to do everything I can to embarrass my kid, too. Hey, I gotta get back at somebody for all this torture.

CHAPTER TWENTY

"I thought you had the bus money your mother gave us," Francis said to Finley. "That's why I appointed you financial director of the Francis Rescue Team."

"Where do you think those Twinkies came from?" Joe asked as Francis stuffed one into his mouth.

"Twinkuhs don cosh that mush," Francis tried to reply, his mouth stuffed with golden sponge cake.

"No, but buying lunch for all of us and all that stuff for those girls did," Joe defended.

"They were cute, dude," Francis countered.

"I'm not saying they weren't, but don't blame me that we're broke."

"Look," the bus driver said, his hands gripping the wheel, "this is all very interesting to me and the other passengers, but you gotta pay to ride on this bus."

Francis reached into his backpack.

"In something *other* than Twinkies," the bus driver said before Francis could pull out his hand.

Francis thought. These were the moments that he lived for, when the odds were against him, the enemy was hostile and time was of the essence. In less time than it took Dewey to break every new toy he got for Christmas, Francis formulated a strategy to get him and the other cadets a free bus ride anyplace the four-wheeled smog mobile was going.

"Sir," Francis began, leaning in to the driver to speak in a hushed tone. "Being that the current situation has taken a unforeseen turn, I am forced to disclose the true nature of our mission."

"You are, are you?" the driver responded, raising a brow.

"We are a crack team of military commandos traveling to the White House to stop an evil plot against the President of these great United States. To say any more would endanger the lives of you and everyone on the bus."

"Well!" the bus driver gasped, wiping his brow. "I had no idea!"

The driver punched the gas pedal and the bus pulled away, leaving Francis and his crack team of military commandos standing at the curb. Francis shook his fist and yelled, "If the President dies, it's on *your* head, mister!"

"So what now," Finley asked.

Francis looked around. They were about a million miles from nowhere and about two million away from anyplace else. They had two boxes of Twinkies, four Slim Jims, and the phone numbers of six girls who "promised" Francis and the other cadets a "fun time" if they were ever in that corner of Dullsville again.

Most people would've given up. Reese would've broken something, Dewey would've stuck Twinkie filling up his nose, and even I would've been at a loss. But not Francis. That's what makes him so cool. He huddled the despondent troops.

"We're broke. Food rations are low and we've met every cute girl this town has to offer. There's only one thing we can do," Francis said, surveying each of their faces. "Find a pool hall."

Luckily for Francis, a pool hall wasn't far. And even luckier for Francis, he won all the games using their bent cues. It's always good to win when you bet a kidney. I totally have no idea what those sailors would've done with a kidney and I don't want to know.

Ever.

CHAPTER TWENTY-ONE

█'m really beginning to realize, even though those IQ tests said I was smarter than everyone else, it's really just a matter of everyone else being stupider than me. Don and Delores certainly weren't doing anything to shatter that argument.

They had been bickering about what to do. Don wanted to dig a tunnel out of the neighborhood from our backyard and Delores wanted to make the police fly in a movie director from Hollywood.

In the end, they decided it was best to barricade the front door. Hey, don't ask me, I'm just the hostage.

With Don and Delores finally too busy to notice me, I went to my room to begin Operation Get Me Outta Here. This was the perfect opportunity to ditch out down my bedsheet ladder. I gave one final look downstairs. Don and Delores were struggling to push the refrigerator in front of the door.

Cool. There were enough frozen TV dinners in that thing to make it weigh a ton. They'd be pushing until next summer. I bolted to the closet for my bedsheet ladder.

"And where do you think you're going?" a voice said behind me.

I turned and saw Reese standing in the door.

"I'm getting out of here," I said. "I have movie tickets."

"Technically, they're Mom's and I'm reclaiming them for her," Reese added, pulling the sheets away from my grabbing hand.

"I don't care if you stay here. You can escape with Don and Delores and live a life on the run. Go ahead. I won't stop you," I blurted out. "Just let *me* leave."

"It's not going to happen," Reese insisted. "If I let a brainiac like you out there, I know Mom and Dad'll make you come up with a plan to save me. Dude, do you realize 'Malibu Co-ed Bikini Beach Party' is on cable tonight!"

"Trust me, Reese, the *last* thing I would want to do is save you. I'm out of here."

"No way. I know this won't last forever, but for now, I am king."

"You're a hostage!" I spat back.

"Then I'm king hostage."

Like I need this? Like my life isn't trouble enough?

I lunged for the window, but Reese grabbed me. We both fell to the floor and wrestled. Reese and I wrestle a lot, and usually the only thing at risk is whether or not Mom would send us to our room.

But this time it was important. I swear the fate of

the world hung in the balance. Okay, maybe not the fate of the world, but definitely the fate of my getting to see *Predatory Aliens 6.*

Reese rolled over me and slugged me in the shoulder.

"Ow!" I yelped.

Reese ran to close the window and found himself staring into Dad's face.

Dad?

"What're you doing out there?" Reese asked.

"Your mother and I are here to rescue you!" Dad replied.

Now I joined Reese at the window.

"Hal! Hal!" we heard Mom say in a hushed tone. "What are you doing?"

"Saving the boys, dear."

Mom stormed out from another bush and looked up at Reese and me.

"I can't believe you boys tried to kill your father!" She hissed.

"We didn't see him!" I explained.

"What were you doing in the tree, Dad?" Reese asked.

"He was trying to save you two! And this is how you ingrates thank him? Do you realize how many children don't even have fathers who would try to save them from criminals, let alone be home every Sunday for family dinner?" Mom said as she searched for Dad in the bushes.

I have no idea what saving us has to do with Sunday dinners, but I think the real reason Dad's there every Sunday is to Heimlich one of us if we choke on Mom's defrosted food loaf.

"Where are you, Hal? Moan or something so I can find you!"

"Oooooooo . . ." My dad complied.

"Mom! I was trying to escape and Reese stopped me!"

"I did not!" Reese protested. "I caught you ruining Mom's sheets and tried to stop you!"

"You're lying, dipwad! Why would I tie Mom's sheets together unless I was trying to escape?"

"How do I know? *You're* the genius."

"Mom! Tell Reese to let me escape!"

"Mom! Tell Malcolm to stop being a baby!"

"Both of you shut up and go to your room! You're both grounded for trying to kill your father!" Mom yelled. She had finally found Dad and helped him to stand.

"Mom! We weren't trying to —"

But my protest was cut short by the "Silent Finger." You know, the single finger that shoots up from the hand. It just points to the sky, but it's saying "If I hear one more word outta you, I won't just be pointing at the sky." There is no way you can combat the Silent Finger. The only thing more powerful is the Don't-You-Even-Think-About-It Stare.

So now I'm grounded? I'm already a hostage, so even if the police save me, I can't leave the house? What's that all about?

"I'm okay, honey. I'm okay," Dad assured her as they shuffled back to the street. My bedsheet ladder dragged behind Dad like a piece of toilet paper stuck to his shoe.

"Did I save the children?" he asked, looking around to see if Reese and I were following them.

CHAPTER TWENTY-TWO

The pigs didn't mind. As long as they had their slop and a little mud, everything was cool.

It was the chickens. It was *always* the chickens. They had began clucking like little feathered tornadoes the moment Francis and the three other cadets had climbed into the back of the farmer's truck. It made what was already a stinky ride even more miserable with the screeching noise of frightened fowl.

"Remind me to become a vegetarian," Francis said, unable to decide whether he should plug his nose or his ears.

Between the noise and the smell, that trip must've been like riding with ten Reeses and fifteen Deweys. If you ask me, having one of each is bad enough.

"How much money do we have left?" Eric asked.

Francis reached into his pocket and pulled out a wadded-up five-dollar bill. "One Abe Lincoln."

"Did you have to pick 'Old MacDonald' to give us a ride?" Finley whined, throwing a look at Francis as a pig bumped him in the head.

"I could've gotten us a ride in a nice air-conditioned

bus if Joe hadn't lost all the money I won playing pool!" Francis defended.

"I didn't lose," Joe defended. "I *gave*."

"Gave. Lost. Burned. What's the difference? We're still riding first class with Peter Porker and his Fantastic Farm Friends," Francis replied.

"I mean the guy said he could get me a deal on a new car," Joe continued, as if anyone in the truck cared to hear his defense again. "How was I supposed to know he'd just steal the money?"

"The guy was pushing around a shopping cart that said SAVE THE DAFFODILS!"

"So?" Joe defended. "I like daffodils."

"I say we just head back to the Academy. This whole mission is a bust," Eric complained. "Maybe Spangler doesn't know we're gone yet. We could —"

"Are you kidding?" Francis shot back. "Spangler knows when a raisin's missing from his Raisin Bran. Besides, my family needs me. I may be my brothers' only hope."

"But your mom and dad are there."

"You're right," Francis realized. "I *am* their only hope."

"Old MacDonald" pulled the truck into a gas station. The brakes squealed and the truck lurched to a stop, sending a chicken flapping into Francis' face.

"Get off me, you winged McNugget!"

As the farmer pumped gas, Francis and the other cadets climbed from the back of the mobile zoo.

"How y'all doin' back there?" the farmer asked.

"Besides the noise, the smell, and the animals, it's the best ride I ever had," Francis offered, picking chicken feathers from his collar.

"Yep, them there aminals sure do can get frenply on ya."

A chill ran down Francis' spine and he decided maybe it was best to never get back in that truck again. Not that I can blame him. I mean, if a farm animal isn't on a patty coated in batter or with a side of dipping sauce, I want nothing to do with it.

Francis looked around the desolate highway 60-whatever gas stop. Things were getting better though. The last time Francis had stretched his legs, he was a million miles from nowhere. Now, he was only about half-a-million miles from nowhere.

Francis had always told me, it's important to know when you're in over your head. And when you are, blame it on someone else and find the closest exit. Problem was, the only exit around here was the one to the bathroom.

Francis kicked an empty can and went over his options. No cash. No pool hall. No car. Pigs. Chickens. Old MacDonald. Just when Francis thought he was doomed to be a roosting post for future KFC extra crispy wings, salvation pulled up to a pump in a pink Cadillac convertible.

"Can you boys pump gas?" a blond girl in the car from Francis's heaven asked.

"Not only can we pump gas," Francis immediately offered, leaping to meet the opportunity, "but we can safely escort you four fine ladies to any destination of your choosing."

"Anyplace?" A brunette asked from the backseat. "Anyplace."

"Well, we're heading down to Florida," the redhead in the passenger seat said.

"What an amazing coincidence!" Francis pretended to be shocked and dropped his mouth open. "Me and my three friends are going in that exact same direction."

"Francis," Finley said, leaning in to whisper, "your house is in the opposite direction."

"I know. I know," Francis whispered back. "But who would you rather ride with? Chicks or chickens? Besides, how bad can they really need me? My mom and dad are there."

Eric finished pumping the gas and the Cadillac raced away.

"So what do you boys do?" the girl with the black hair asked.

"Movies," Francis said without a moment's hesitation. "We produce movies."

CHAPTER TWENTY-THREE

"If Batman is Batman, why isn't Robin Robin-man?"

Officer Williams sighed. He ran his fingers through his hair and took a deep breath, trying his best to maintain his patience.

"Look," he said. "I'm only going over this one more time. Robin was the *Boy Wonder*. He was Robin, the Boy Wonder. He was a kid, not a man. A kid."

Dewey thought about this for a second, then continued, "So why isn't he the Kid Wonder?"

Officer Williams raised his finger to hush Dewey. "No more! No more Batman questions. No more about Robin. And no more about Alfred the butler. If I have to answer one more question about Alfred I'm gonna —" Officer Williams stopped.

He looked around for someone to help him, but all the other officers had cleared a Dewey-free zone around the poor man. Dewey had worked his way through twelve officers before he was handed over to Williams. Each of them was a well-trained law enforcement professional skilled at handling pressure, exposing themselves to life-threatening situations, and protecting the city from all kinds of scum and dangerous people.

Against Dewey, the poor souls never had a chance.

As Dewey took a deep breath to start a new round of irritation, Officer Williams did the only thing he could to save what few scraps of his sanity remained.

"Roberts! Roberts!" Officer Williams called out to the unsuspecting rookie who had just shown up for his shift.

"Yessir?" Roberts asked, climbing out of his car.

"Chief Klemp wants you to watch the boy," Officer Williams said and thrust Dewey into Roberts's arms.

"But I was supposed to —"

"No! You've been reassigned. Trust me."

Officer Williams cracked a wild smile and ran off like a kid released from detention. Roberts smiled at Dewey.

"So, what's your name little —"

Roberts stopped in mid-sentence and flinched. A foul scent stabbed at his nose.

"Mommy says I'm gassy," Dewey said sheepishly.

Inside the house, Delores was "entertaining" us with a selection of songs from movies I hope I never see. Reese and I were forced to sit on the couch and clap at all the appropriate times, which was, like, every thirty seconds.

"Maybe escaping isn't such a bad idea," Reese whispered to me.

Wasn't this what I'd been saying? Right now I

could be watching aliens eating other aliens. Better than that? I could be watching Krelboynes cowering in fear behind their popcorn. Instead? I'm listening to Delores try to remember the words to some stupid love song. One thing I know? There's no love song in *Predatory Aliens* 6.

CHAPTER TWENTY-FOUR

Everything was going nowhere fast. Between Don, Delores, and Reese, it just didn't seem like I was going to be able to make my escape. Then I realized, the best way to escape was to take matters into my own hands.

"Don't you think it's time we ended this?" I asked Don. "I mean, what do you want? Ever since you've got here, the only thing you've accomplished was getting an interview and four pizzas — and those were *my* ideas."

"And getting rid of Dewey," Don added. "Don't forget that."

Yeah. *That'll* be an accomplishment everyone will be speaking about for decades to come.

"But what do you guys *want*? What are your demands?" I explained. "Hostage-takers without demands are just . . . teachers."

"What're you saying?" Don questioned, standing from the window. "You think . . . are you saying . . . we should ask for more pizzas?"

"No! I'm saying think big picture here. Did you plan on staying here forever?"

"Well, this *is* a nice neighborhood," Delores replied.

"And what about the police?" I asked.

"They gotta go home sometime!" Delores offered.

I swear, this was like explaining gravity to Reese. No matter how hard you try, regardless of how small the words are or how simple you draw the pictures, in the end it's just best to say it's magic.

"Okay," I said, pulling out a piece of paper and pen. "Here's what you're going to read to the police."

"Sounds like a perfect plan!" Don enthused.

"'Cept'n that I can't read."

"Okay," I said, pulling out a second piece of paper. "Here's what *I'm* going to read to the police."

I thought about it for a few moments. I quickly made some notes and a brief outline of "Don's" statement.

"Whatcha got?" Delores asked, peeking over my shoulder.

"Okay, this is it," I read. "Don and Delores have issued the following demands to be met within one hour in exchange for Malcolm."

"What about me?" Reese asked, joining the group.

"You stay with them as a hostage to assure safe transport to their chartered jet."

"Cool," Reese agreed. "More chance of seeing a gunfight at the airport."

"Guns!?" Don gasped. "We don't have no guns!"

"What?" I asked.

"I said we don't have no guns!" Don repeated.

"What?" I asked again.

Don could have repeated that sentence a hundred

times and each time I would have said the same thing. "What?" I mean, what else *could* I say? I've been sitting in this house like a rat in a lab cage and the only thing Don's had to stop me is his bad breath?

"No guns?" Reese spat. "You guys stink."

"How did you get the clerk to give you all that money at the liquor store? What have you been threatening us with?" I had to know.

"Don was shoplifting fudgesicles," Delores confessed. "For our late-afternoon snack. He loves anything on a stick. Don had shoved one in his pocket and the clerk thought it was a gun."

Don jabbed his hand into his pocket and immediately pulled it out covered in sticky, fudgy goo. "There's still some left," he said, licking his fingers.

Reese raised an eyebrow as Don poked his hand back into his pocket. "Don't even think about it," Don said to Reese. "This baby's *allll* mine."

Suddenly, the front door never looked so big. But even if they didn't have guns, I couldn't just walk out. I mean, Don was bigger than me and if he wanted me to stay he could just tackle me — and if he didn't, you can bet Reese would. Don had already agreed to let me read the list of demands to the police. All I needed to do was wait until I went outside to read the list, then just keep walking.

"There won't be any gunfights," I assured them. "We'll give the police your demands and get this whole stupid thing over with."

"Should we rehearse?" Delores asked. "I'm much better if I rehearse."

"Just look dangerous," I returned.

Delores stood and scowled. "How's this?"

So she looked more constipated than dangerous, but there aren't enough hours left in my poor short life for her to learn how to act.

"Terrifying," I lied. "Now let's go over the list. Demand One: $100,000 in non-sequential unmarked bills. Two: A leading role for Delores in a movie. Three: A private jet to take you to Brazil, which is a non-extradition country. Four: The government must acknowledge the WWF wrestlers are aliens."

Everyone looked at me like *I* was an alien.

"You *always* make one crazy demand so you can plead insanity if they catch you."

"Gotcha!" Don shook his head and laughed. "Brazil. That's just nutty."

So there you have it. I'm at the mercy of a goofball whose lone threat is his ability to smear chocolate on me. And this time, I'm not talking about Dewey.

I'm serious about walking out the front door – or maybe the back door since the fridge is propped against the front one – and then just keeping on walking. I can finally get out of the house without having to blow up something in the kitchen first.

Although that might be cool to do anyway.

So I was about to pick up the list and wave "hasta la vista" to the whole lot of 'em, when I see Don and Delores listening to some Reese story about pouring pudding over a Krelboyne's head last week in school.

Then it hit me. I can't leave these two at the mercy of Reese. I swear that Don's IQ has been deteriorating at a rapid pace since his initial encounter with my brother Slug-a-lot. Science has yet to prove that prolonged exposure to Reese does not have adverse side-effects besides a rash.

And on top of that, as much as I want to leave, I can't. Who knows, they might be lying about the guns.

Yeah, that's it. They might be.

Sure.

CHAPTER TWENTY-FIVE

I stood with a piece of paper in my hand. With all the police and TV news lights shining in my face, I felt like I was totally staring into the sun.

"... A private jet to take them to Brazil, and the government must acknowledge that the WWF wrestlers are aliens." I lowered the list and looked at the blinding glare of the arc lights. I hoped somebody was still out there.

"Brazil?" Chief Klemp said, slapping his forehead. "These people are nuts!"

"You bet they are, mister, and you've done nothing to save my children!" Mom shouted at him. I couldn't see her, but with a voice like hers, you really don't need to.

"That's right, lady, because I've been too busy trying to deal with you, first!" Chief Klemp yelled back at Mom.

"In case you haven't noticed, Chief, you are a public servant and I am the public!" Mom countered.

"I know the song and dance. I hear it from your kind all the time."

"My kind?! *My kind?!* And what exactly *is* my kind, Chief Klemp? Could you please tell me that?"

I thought Chief Klemp was a smart guy. I mean, being chief and all you'd think he could figure out what's what. You'd think. See, with my mom, sometimes the best answer is to not answer at all. I'm sure if someone had explained that to Chief Klemp, he wouldn't have said the things he said and that I will no way repeat — I've got enough trouble as it is. Let's just say you can't even hear this stuff in a movie unless accompanied by someone over eighteen — or unless you sneak in.

The part I *will* repeat is the end. Pure "G-rated." Chief Klemp leaned closer to my mom's face and finished, "But I'll probably get a medal for having to deal with you!"

"You haven't even *begun* to deal with me!"

The last time Mom said that, she ended up with 100 hours of community service. The way things were going, she was going to get arrested before Don and Delores. I knew when it was time to go someplace safer . . . like back in the house.

That was when the FBI finally arrived. A couple of the FBI agents came up to Mom and Chief Klemp as they argued. One of them must've been carrying a tear gas gun because the next thing I know, Mom had grabbed one from somewhere and I saw her running toward the house.

I swear it's true! I couldn't make this stuff up. Who would believe me? Heck, I'm watching it and *I* don't believe me.

The police and FBI agents chased after her, but it

was too late. She fired the gun, but get this, the tear gas canister totally missed our house and smashed through our neighbor's window.

The last thing I saw before I closed the door was the police wrestling my mom to the ground. The Davis family stumbled out from their house, coughing and gagging. Tears poured down their faces like their eyeballs were showerheads.

"What's going on out there?" Delores asked.

"Nothing much. I think my mom just got arrested for gassing the neighbors."

"That'll teach the Davises to mess with her," Reese chortled.

"I really like it here, baby. Wouldn't it be nice to have a place like this and all?" Delores asked Don, cuddling up to him on the couch.

"I don't think we can, sweetheart," Don replied. "Malcolm's sending us to Brazil."

Sending them? They made it sound like I'm punishing them! When did they become the victims and I become the adult in all this?

"Can't we stay, Don. Do we have to go?" Delores laid her cheek against Don's chest.

"I don't know, Delores. Malcolm seems set on Brazil," Don sighed.

Enough is enough. I had tried to end this with words, but it was time to take action. I mean, Don and Delores take me hostage and now I'm the one feeling guilty because they don't want to leave — like I said, "Hey come into my house and take me hostage. Then the police will surround the house until my parents go crazy."

Although now that I think about it? My parents were already crazy.

"Where you going?" Reese asked as I headed up the stairs.

"To my room."

"Don't think about tying our blue jeans together to make a rope," he informed me, holding up a pair of scissors. "I already cut all the legs off. And if you see Mom or Dad in the tree again, ask them for the cable lock codes . . . for Don and Delores, of course."

I flicked on the computer in my room, dialed up the Internet and spent a few minutes searching. His last name was all I needed.

The great thing about the Internet is that you can pretty much find anyone anywhere in the world *and* sign up for a low-interest credit card with a mere click of the mouse.

Not that I had time to sign up for a credit card. Besides, I think most of the credit companies were on to me by now.

Anyway, I got the phone number I needed, signed off and dialed the number. The phone rang several times before a woman answered.

"Hello," I said. "You don't know me, ma'am, but my name is Malcolm . . ."

CHAPTER TWENTY-SIX

It had been thirty-minutes since I made the call. Or should I say *the* call? It went pretty well and now I was sitting in the kitchen waiting for D day. Reese was in the living room trying to figure out the five-digit code to the cable channel lock. He was up to 00671, so that only left him 99,328 more combinations to try.

Hey, to see "Malibu Co-ed Bikini Beach Party," even *I* think it's time well-spent.

"Malcolm," Delores said from the doorway, "mind if I join you?"

Uh, yes. Go away. Leave me alone. Don't sing to me.

"Sure!" Why am I so nice?

"Reese says you're real smart-like."

Compared to Reese, everyone is "real smart-like."

"I guess Don and I don't always do smart things," Delores continued.

Hello! Welcome to the understatement of the decade!

"But I guess, when you're in love as much as we are, just trying to stay together is sometimes the smartest thing you can do, y'know?"

"I guess," I said, not really knowing because, one, I'm not in love and, two, if I were I sure wouldn't be sitting in a kitchen with a liquor store thief.

Delores smiled at me. "I just wanted to thank you for helping us."

"I was trying to get out of here," I replied, wanting to be honest. "That's all."

"But Don told you we don't have guns. We couldn't really stop you from leaving."

"Look, if you're trying to say that I only stayed here to help you . . . you're, like, totally wrong. Why in the world would I ever stay just to help you and Don?"

"But you did."

"I had a very good reason to stay."

"Like what?"

"Stop confusing me!" I protested.

"I'll tell you why you stayed, Malcolm," Delores continued, standing to leave the kitchen. "Because you're a good egg."

A good egg? She makes it sound like I was left under Dewey's bed by the Easter Bunny or something. I'm just a kid who for some reason stayed when the only thing stopping him was the melted remains of a frozen dessert treat. And that reason was . . . I stayed because . . . see there's a real good explanation for all of this.

I don't know. I guess it's just kinda like Spider-Man. I mean, sure he could've used that whole spider-power thing to make cash, but he helped people instead. I'm not saying I have superpowers —

although it would be cool to shoot webs outta your hands. Do you know how hard it is to meet someone whose life is more pathetic than mine and isn't a Krelboyne? Sometimes when you've got things better off than other people, does it really hurt to help them a little?

"It was nice to be a part of a family again," Delores added, stopping in the doorway. "If only for a little while."

"Even mine?" I asked.

"Especially yours."

Wow. What just happened? That was more surprising than Reese passing math class. And what is that totally weird feeling that's going on in me right now? I mean, do I feel . . . lucky?

Suddenly there was a loud voice booming through the bullhorn. I know this is gonna be surprising: it *wasn't* my mom, but it was someone's.

"Donnie! Donnie Lindstrom!" the voice shouted. "Exactly what do you think you're doing?"

In the living room, Don leaped from the couch like his butt was spring-loaded. "Momma?!"

Yep. You got it. I had called Don's mom. I knew that if she was even one-tenth of my mom, this whole thing would end in under five minutes.

"You march your butt out here right now and let these nice policemen arrest you!" Mrs. Lindstrom shouted into the bullhorn.

"Aww, Momma," Don whined from the window. "I got hostages and demands."

"You have no such thing!" his mother yelled back, lowering the bullhorn. "You have inconvenienced this lovely woman, and we'll have no more of this nonsense."

Lovely woman? I looked out the window to see who Mrs. Lindstrom was talking about. Get this, it was *my* mom. Suddenly Don's intelligence was making a lot more sense to me.

Don stomped his feet and balled his fists. Delores walked up to him and gave him a big hug. "Come on, baby," she said. "Let's go home."

"Aww, sweetie, I'm sorry you won't get that movie role Malcolm demanded for us."

"It's okay," Delores assured him. "Besides, some-one will have to play me in the Movie-of-the-Week. This'll give me plenty of time to rehearse."

Yeah, about three to five years with good behavior.

I watched Don and Delores open the door and dis-appear in the blinding lights of the police cars like ghosts fading away in a dream. As quickly as they had stormed through our front door and taken us hostage, they were gone, replaced by the grateful hugs and kisses of Mom and Dad.

And that was that.

At least until Mom saw the inside of the house.

By ten o'clock Saturday morning, things were pretty much back to normal. Of course, Mom still wouldn't let me go see Predatory Aliens 6 even though I claimed this should be my reward for surviving.

She thinks any movie where someone gets eaten can only rot your brain. She obviously doesn't understand, that's the point!

I had some time to kill before the movie started. You'd think I'd spend it creating some excuse why it was imperative that she let me go see it, but I couldn't stop thinking about the whole night.

Mom fighting off the police force, Dad climbing trees to save us. I don't know. Maybe they don't know how much they embarrass me because they just think about how much they love me instead. Wow, does that sound

Weird or what? Forget I even suggested it.

But I guess Delores is right. Being a part of a family is nice. Sometimes great. Even if it's mine.

And speaking of family, I just got a call from Francis. Seems he needed a couple of thousand dollars to bail himself outta some prison in Canada.

"Why are you in Canada?" I asked.

"Cause that's where the airplane landed," he said.

As long as it makes sense to him.